Boston Skyline from
Boston Harbor

AuthorHouse™
1663 Liberty Drive
Bloomington, IN 47403
www.authorhouse.com
Phone: 1-800-839-8640

First published by AuthorHouse   2/16/2010

ISBN: 978-1-4389-9249-5 (sc)

Library of Congress Control Number: 2009913908

Printed in the United States of America
Bloomington, Indiana

This book is printed on acid-free paper.

authorHOUSE®

In the last decade Boston has undergone a metamorphosis known to all her inhabitants as the Big Dig. Essentially, it was an engineering and planning feat to improve the entrance/egress and movement of the traffic through the city in a more efficient manner. It also led to some wonderful fallout such as the new parks and open areas for recreation. After years of ongoing construction and constant rerouting of traffic, we now have a third harbor tunnel to the airport, and a depressed artery, which takes you underground through the city from Chinatown to the new iconic Zakim bridge, at what was once the Garden at North Station. The idea for this children's tale was born from a story on the nightly news back in the very beginning of this undertaking. I pencilled in my idea for the book then and tried it out on my then toddler grandaughter. I approached my friend and Occupational Therapy colleague, who is a wonderful photographer, asking if she would help illustrate the story with some of her images of Boston. Then life happened, and the project, despite erratic attempts to revive it, got put on the back burner. Alison and I have since retired, and my first grandaughter has just celebrated her 13th birthday. It is time to chronicle The Big Dig in a way that children growing up then and now can relate to. Boston has managed to integrate the old, it's historical heritage, and the new into a harmonious fabric which is uniquely Boston. The Big Dig, for all it's organized chaos and almost indeterminate length is now an important piece of Boston's history and heritage.

Priscilla

← *John Hancock and the Trinity Church*

This book is dedicated to
my grandaughters Juliana and Samantha
and to my daughter Debbie for her patience and
technical help.

I also want to thank Donna Boisvert
for sharing four of her photos from our Tall Ship
adventure.

P.A.B

Mr. and Mrs. Duckling lived right outside of Boston near the Boston Gas Tank, with the pretty rainbow painted on it.

Dorchester Gas Tank →

Every year when the summer was over and fall began to bring cold evenings, they would fly South for the winter, and return again in the spring.

This year, as they were beginning their flight, Mrs. Duckling saw a billboard right by the underpass at Chinatown. It said something about being patient with the Big Dig.

She asked Mr. Duckling,
"What on earth is the Big Dig?"
He explained that the Southeast Expressway
could no longer handle all the cars that came to
Boston every day, and that the road was going
to be rebuilt.

Men were going to dig a third harbor tunnel to the airport and the main road was going to go underground, beneath where Rowes Wharf is, and come out at a beautiful new bridge.

Rowes Wharf →

"It's all going to take years to do" he said. He also said he didn't think it would matter much to them, as they flew, rather than drove, wherever they needed to go.

When spring was in the air and it was time to return to Boston, Mrs. Duckling was anxious to get home and settled because she was expecting a new family.

Mr. Duckling was going to be delayed because he had *been* chosen to help the grandma and grandpa ducks, who tended to be a bit slower, to get home safely.

The Ducklings agreed that Mrs. Duckling should go ahead to the old nesting ground. After all, she couldn't get too lost with the big rainbow tank to mark her way.

When Mrs. Duckling got home, she couldn't believe her eyes! There were piles of dirt and tall cranes and lots of big yellow earth moving machines everywhere!

She found a place to nest not too far from the water's edge and just hoped that Mr. Duckling would get home soon.

Every morning the men in the yellow hats would come and move the piles of dirt with their big yellow machines.

It was noisy and dirty, but Mrs. Duckling couldn't leave because soon she had five new baby ducklings to care for.

Ike and Mike and Joe were supposed to move the dirt to right where the ducklings were nested.

One bright and sunny morning Joe was driving one of the big yellow machines and pushing a huge pile of dirt down toward a gully by the water's edge. Mrs. Duckling was busy lining up her ducklings when she saw a wall of moving dirt coming right toward them! She froze!!!!!!!!

Just in the nick of time, she heard a loud whistle and everything stopped.

Joe jumped down from the machine and took his lunchbox to a nearby rock. As he sat down to have his morning coffee and donut, out of the corner of his eye he saw Mrs. Duckling march her fuzzy little babies down to the water for their swimming lesson and then back to the gully where he had almost dumped tons of heavy brown earth!

Joe got Ike and Mike and told them what he had seen.

They talked and decided to try to put off the dirt moving near the water until after the ducklings had moved on, but they wouldn't be able to wait too long!

Every day the ducklings went to the water and one by one learned how to swim. But everyday they had to return to the nest because Enid, the littlest one, just couldn't learn to swim by herself. Ike and Mike and Joe were worried because they couldn't wait much longer.

Finally, Enid got the hang of swimming, and Mrs. Duckling decided they should swim out to Thompson Island, where there were no yellow earth moving machines.

Thompson Island →

Mr. and Mrs. Duckling had talked long ago about an emergency plan that meant meeting up at Thompson Island, across the water from the stately J.F.K. Library, if anything ever went wrong.

John F. Kennedy
PRESIDENTIAL LIBRARY AND MUSEUM

The next morning, Joe found that the ducks had moved and Ike and Mike began to move the waiting piles of earth to the water's edge.

After one more week, Mr. Duckling returned to the old nesting ground near the Big Gas Tank. He knew at a glance that things were not right and after circling around without finding Mrs. Duckling, he remembered the emergency plan and flew out to Thompson Island.

He found his new family and said he knew of a wonderful new home for them where they would always be safe. He had heard about it years ago from some of the older ducks.

George Washington Monument at entrance to Boston Public Garden →

"It has beautiful flowers, boats that look like giant swans, and lots of children who bring bread and crackers to feed the ducks in the pond" he said.

Swan Boat - Boston Public Garden →

So once Father Duckling was assured that his new family could fly as well as swim, he gathered them altogether and headed into Boston. They circled over the golden dome of the State House, descended over the frog pond in the Common and landed in the Boston Public Garden.

State House, Frog Pond at Boston Common and Boston Public Garden sign →

And that is how the Duckling family came to live in the Boston Public Garden, because of the Big Dig.

Suspension bridge at the Boston Public Garden →

The End

Zakim Bridge from the North end photo by Donna B →

LaVergne, TN USA
05 March 2010
175075LV00001B